THICKER THAN WATER

THICKER THAN WATER

Natasha Deen

orca soundings

ORCA BOOK PUBLISHERS

Library and Archives Canada Cataloguing in Publication

Deen, Natasha, author
Thicker than water / Natasha Deen.
(Orca soundings)

Issued in print and electronic formats.
ISBN 978-1-4598-2198-9 (softcover).—ISBN 978-1-4598-2199-6 (PDF).—
ISBN 978-1-4598-2200-9 (EPUB)

I. Title. II. Series: Orca soundings
PS8607.E444T55 2019   jc813'.6   C2018-904892-1
C2018-904893-X

First published in the United States, 2019
Library of Congress Control Number: 2018954097

Summary: In this high-interest novel for teens, Zack has
to decide between betraying a family member or losing a
friend when an eighteen-year-old girl goes missing.

MIX
Paper from
responsible sources
FSC® C016245

*Orca Book Publishers is dedicated to preserving the environment and
has printed this book on Forest Stewardship Council® certified paper.*

Orca Book Publishers gratefully acknowledges the support for its
publishing programs provided by the following agencies: the Government of
Canada, the Canada Council for the Arts and the Province of British Columbia
through the BC Arts Council and the Book Publishing Tax Credit.

Edited by Tanya Trafford
Cover images by Shutterstock.com/Realstock (front) and
Shutterstock.com/Krasovski Dmitri (back)

ORCA BOOK PUBLISHERS
orcabook.com

Printed and bound in Canada.

22 21 20 19 • 4 3 2 1

For Sven

Chapter One

I don't hear the car come up the driveway. But when the doorbell rings, I just know it's a cop on the other side. He pushes the button again, and the sound crackles through me.

"Zack, honey, can you get that?" Mom calls from the kitchen.

My muscles won't work.

"Zack, now!"

I jump up from the couch and stumble to the door. I nod at the officer, grateful my long hair hangs over my eyes. I don't want him to see the fear in them. It's a weird thing, wanting him here at the same time I wish he'd go away. "Hi, Detective Tyron."

"Hi, Zack. Are your folks home?"

When I nod, he pushes his bulk through the doorway and stands in the hall.

"Uh, my mom's here." I close the door, then flick my hair out of my face. "Mom!" I call. "A cop wants to talk to you."

"Actually, buddy, it's you I want to talk to. But you're only seventeen, so I need your mom around."

Does he know that I know more about Ella's disappearance than I'm admitting? "Oh, yeah, sure. Come into the kitchen." I smile back at him, but it's not a real smile.

Mom wipes her hands on a dish towel. The question is in her eyes.

"Detective Tyron." The officer holds out his hand.

She takes it. "Rabia Bernard."

"I'm one of the leads on the Ella Larson case."

My mom's face crumples. "So it's official? She really is missing?"

"The only thing we know for sure is that she's been out of contact with her friends and family for twenty-four hours." Detective Tyron pauses. "And that's unusual for her."

"More than unusual," says Mom. "She and her mom are inseparable." She wipes invisible crumbs off the table. "Did she take off? Did—" Mom glances at me. "Did someone hurt her?"

"We don't know all the facts yet, ma'am," he says. "It's Ella's first year at university. Sometimes that kind of freedom goes to a kid's head.

Especially when they're no longer in the same city as their parents. They're traveling, partying and not checking in with Mom and Dad. Other times it could be something more serious—" Detective Tyrone spreads his hands. "I wouldn't feel right if I didn't explore every possibility."

Mom nods toward the table. "Please sit down. Can I get you some coffee?" She looks my way and sighs. "Zack, the hair."

I yank it back into a ponytail.

"Thank you," the detective says to Mom as he sits. "That would be great. Black, please."

"How is the investigation going?"

"We do have some leads we're following up on. Yesterday Zack and his dad stopped by and gave me a statement."

"Yes," says Mom. She pops a pod into the coffee machine, slides a mug into the tray and pushes the Start button. "They told me."

"So you're a full day into the investigation, and you don't know anything," I say.

"Zack!" Mom smiles weakly at the detective, then glares at me.

"Well, it's true, isn't it?" I ask. "And aren't the first twenty-four hours the most important? One of the shows I watch said the longer a case takes, the harder it is to solve."

"Zack wants to be a detective when he grows up," says my mom. "He's taking a criminology class at school. And he's obsessed with crime shows." She glares at me again. "But his manners could use some work."

"It's fine," Detective Tyron says. "I understand how worried he must be about his friend."

He turns to look at me. "Your school offers a criminology class?"

"Yeah," I say. "It's pretty cool. We're studying serial killers right now."

Mom rolls her eyes. "He's convinced his father that watching those violent crime shows is part of his homework."

"They *are*," I insist. "*Crime Scene Hunters* is all about looking for clues and paying attention to people. That's how you find out the truth."

Mom snorts. "This from the kid who thought the shadow of his bedroom lamp was a man coming into his room to kidnap him."

"I was ten!"

"I still don't like you filling your head with all those horrible images of dead bodies."

"If I'm going to be a cop—" I stop when I realize Detective Tyron is watching me. He doesn't need to listen to the same fight I've had with my mom a million times. "I'm not a kid."

Detective Tyron coughs. "I think it's great that you're thinking about getting into law enforcement. Our force is always looking for new recruits."

"We'll see," says Mom. "So what *do* you know about Ella's disappearance, Detective Tyron?"

"Not as much as I'd like. Her transit pass was used to get on the subway at Yonge Street Station," he says. "We're trying to figure out where she got off." He frowns. "But Toronto is a big city. It's a lot of ground to cover."

"What about the cameras at the station?" I ask.

For a moment there's only the sound of the coffee machine.

"A missing kid." Mom gives me a wobbly smile. "It's a parent's worst night-mare." The last of the coffee drips into the mug. She hands it to the detective.

"Thank you," he says.

"You're welcome. So how can Zack help you? I'm sure he already told you everything he knows."

Not true.

"Zack, I'd like to go over your day with Ella one more time," he says. "You were the last one to see her."

No, I wasn't. But I can't say that.

"Tell me again what you remember," Detective Tyron says.

"She had a reading break this week. We made plans to meet up after school."

The detective takes out a notebook and pen. "What did you talk about? Did she seem upset?"

"She was stressed out. First year was hard," I say. "She was sure she was failing, but she always thinks that way. I tried to make her feel better, but I'm not sure it worked."

He checks his notes. "I understand she's in pre-med." He looks up as Mom takes the seat beside him. "A smart young lady."

"The apple doesn't fall far from the tree," my mom says. "Her mom, Loni, is a driven woman. It's in the genes."

Detective Tyron flips the page. "Dad's out of the picture?"

"That loser?" Mom makes a face. "Phil got busted for stealing a car. He spent a few years in jail and blew through Loni's savings trying to appeal his sentence. As soon as he got out he divorced Loni. He left her penniless and bailed on the family. That poor woman works three jobs just to make ends meet. No one knows where he is."

That's not true either. I must do something that gives me away, because Detective Tyron says, "Zack, is that true?"

Mom frowns. "Zack, do you know something about Ella's dad?"

I don't want to say anything, but Mom's stare is hard-core.

"They reconnected when Ella went to university," I say.

"Zack!" She stands. "How could you stay quiet about this? Ella's missing and Loni's going out of her mind! Phil might have her, and you never thought to—"

"He didn't do it!"

Detective Tyron pounces on my words. "How do you know?"

Me and my big mouth. "Oh, uh…"

They're both staring at me.

"Her dad doesn't live here. If he'd been in town, she would've told me." *Maybe, maybe not.*

The detective's pen hovers over the paper. "Do you know where Ella's dad is living now?"

I shake my head.

"Let's go over the day you spent with Ella again," he says. "Do you remember anything unusual?"

I close my eyes, trying to think. "No, we walked around. We stopped for lunch at The Java Hut up on Ellesmere." So far, so good. That's all true.

"Then what happened?"

I shrug. "I had to grab some stuff from the mall—"

"Ella didn't go with you?"

"No, we split up after we finished our sandwiches. She said she had an appointment. She didn't tell me what it was." I hear myself rushing the words. I slow down, so I don't give myself away. "At the mall I met up with my friend Ayo—"

He checks his notes. "Ayo Mohammed?"

"Yes. We hung out for a bit. Then I came home."

"That it?" He's staring at me. "Nothing else?"

I meet his gaze, pretend I'm thinking it through. Then I give another shrug. "That's all I remember, Detective."

He holds my gaze for a moment, then looks down and makes another note.

"Did you talk to Ayo?" I ask.

"He's next on my list."

I hear the door open. Dad's home. He walks into the kitchen. His eyebrows go up when he sees us. "Oh. It's Detective Brian—?"

"Tyron." The detective rises and shakes his head. "Just doing some follow-up."

"Okay." Dad drops his bag on the counter.

"Patrick!" Mom shoves the bag onto the floor. "I've told you not to do that. We prepare food on the counter, and your bag is dirty."

"Oh. I thought it was because my bag scratches the surface. No, wait, it's because it's wet." He takes a breath to continue, then realizes Detective Tyron is watching him. "Sorry," he mumbles.

Detective Tyron turns and looks at me, but I look away. It's an old fight, but it's one of a million fights Mom and Dad seem to have all the time now.

"How's the investigation going?" Dad asks.

"Not much so far. Have the kids at school said anything to you?"

Dad shakes his head. "I know I'm the guidance counselor, but the kids are hit or miss when it comes to talking to me. Sometimes they're great. Sometimes I'm one step up from dog poop on the bottom of their shoe."

That's not actually true. He's one of the most popular teachers at our school.

"It's sad," says Dad. "I wish I could help."

It's not the first time he's said that. He said the same thing when we first learned about Ella's disappearance. And he said it when we were at the station yesterday. The knot in my stomach tightens.

Dad *could* help. All he needs to do is open his mouth. As soon as he talks, I can too.

"Are you sure you haven't heard anything more?" Detective Tyron asks. "Sometimes even the tiniest details can help."

I'm holding my breath, silently screaming, *Tell him! Tell him!*

But Dad says, "No, sorry." Then he looks at me and says, "Zack would know more than I do, since he was the last one to see her. Right, Champ?"

He makes eye contact, and I'm sure he wants me to lie. I don't want to, but it must be some kind of West Indian–kid thing to do what your parents say. I hear myself saying, "Yeah, I guess."

But it's not true.

After we said our goodbyes at the café, I saw Ella at the mall. She was in the food court with Dad. He must have been the appointment she had.

Something about the way they were talking made me hang back, then walk away. Later, when I saw her leaving the mall, I ran to catch up to her. I wanted to know what was going on, why she and my dad had been together. I almost lost her in the crowd of people, but then I spotted her jogging toward Dad's car. I saw her get in on the passenger side.

And that was the last time anyone saw her.

Chapter Two

Detective Tyron leaves a few minutes later. I go back to watching TV on the couch and pretending I don't hear the low, angry voices in the kitchen. Why do my parents think I won't know they're fighting? Dinner is silent and tense, which is okay. I need time to figure out a way to talk to Dad about seeing him and Ella at the mall. But by the time dessert's done, I still don't have a plan. I clear the dishes, then head to the family room.

The latest episode of *Crime Scene Hunters* is on, but I can't concentrate. I don't think my dad's a bad guy, but the whole thing makes me uncomfortable. If he has nothing to hide, why didn't he come clean with Detective Tyron?

"Hey, Champ." Dad claps me on the back.

The sudden contact makes me jump.

"Whoa, calm down." He squints at the screen. "Too many dead bodies and secrets for you." He sits down next to me and changes the channel.

"I was watching that."

"When you pay the bills, you can choose what we watch." He settles back onto the couch and zones out, watching the football game on the screen.

"Dad. Dad. Hey…" I snap my fingers. "Dad."

"What?" He keeps his gaze on the game.

"About Ella…"

"Don't worry about her, Champ. I'm sure she'll show up soon. The cops know what they're doing."

"Yeah, I know, but I wanted to talk to you about the day she went missing. We were walking around, and after she left…"

"Uh-huh." His eyes follow the players on the field.

"I met Ayo at the mall."

He freezes. It's just for a split second, and then he says, "Uh-huh." But I can hear the tension in his voice.

"While I was there—"

"You got those shoes on sale. I know. You told me." He waves me off. "I'm watching the game, Champ. Let's talk about this later."

But I need to talk now. The stress is eating at my stomach. "But Dad—"

He lifts the remote and pauses the game. When he turns to look at me, there's a hard light in his eyes. "Look, Zack, I know you're worried about your friend. I know you want to be just like the guys you see on TV, solving crimes and catching bad guys."

He leans in close. I can smell the coffee on his breath.

"Whatever clue you think you might have, forget about it. Whatever you think you saw…" He pauses. "You didn't. Do you hear me? Let the cops do their job. When you've finished school and become a real-life detective, you can join them. But until then keep your nose out of their business." He points at me. "Do we understand each other?"

I fight the sick feeling that's rising inside me. "Yeah, Yeah, we do."

The next day at school Ayo finds me in the empty stairwell during our free period.

"There you are. I thought you were sick or something." He plops down beside me.

"What?" I'm staring out the windows that line the landing. It's a boring view of the front parking lot and lawn, but it helps me zone out.

"Your crime show was on last night. Usually you blow up my phone with all your real-time texting about what's happening in the episode."

"Oh. No, I saw it."

His black eyebrows rise. "That's it? *I saw it*?"

"Yeah. I saw the show. It was fine."

"Since when is anything about—" Ayo slaps his forehead. "Aw, man, I'm an idiot."

"Tell me something I don't know."

He ignores the dig. "It's Ella, isn't it?" He shakes his head. "Of course it is. How can you concentrate on a show when you're worried about her?" His voice softens. "Listen, Ella's smart. I'm sure she's okay. I bet she's just blowing off steam somewhere."

"It feels like more than that," I say. "She hasn't posted anything online in days. She won't return my texts—"

"She was pissed off. You two went at it pretty good."

"Thanks for reminding me."

Ayo winces. "I mean, maybe she needs some space."

"Yeah, maybe. But not answering my texts? That's mean, and Ella's not mean." The sick feeling from last night rises through me again. I want to tell Ayo what I saw. I need someone to tell me I'm crazy for thinking my dad's holding back information. I bet he and

Ella were talking about her university classes or something innocent like that. My dad doesn't know anything that can help the police. That's why he's staying silent.

Right. That makes sense. So why does my gut say there was more to their meeting than a chat about math class?

Just then several vans pull into the school parking lot. I see the local TV-station logo on one of them. Ayo and I stand.

"What's going on?" Ayo says, nose pressed against the window now. "Do you think they found her?"

I shake my head. "If the police had found her, they would do a news conference in front of the station. They wouldn't hold it here."

"Maybe there's been a break in the case."

"Maybe."

Ayo stretches to get a better view. Not that there's much to see. The reporters climb out of their vans and start setting up their cameras. A couple of them form a loose group and start talking.

"Maybe someone in the school has information, and they want to talk to him."

Dad's here. Did the reporters find out something? Are they here to make him explain what he was doing with Ella? The worst-case scenario flashes through my head. My dad, hand-cuffed and shrinking from the cameras. Reporters following me through the streets, shouting, *Did you know about your dad? Why didn't you come forward sooner?*

I don't know what to do. I'm not sure if I should stay here, run away or go warn Dad.

"Look." Ayo points.

Ella's mom is walking up the pathway. She looks horrible but somehow perfectly put together at the same time. She's one of those ladies whose clothes and hair are always just right.

The horrible isn't in her clothes or her hair. Her face looks like she's aged a hundred years in the past two days. And she moves like she's even older. Her steps are slow and painful. She's clutching some sheets of paper.

Mr. Wexford, our school principal, comes down the steps to greet her. He takes her hand and then hugs her. Together they walk over to where the reporters have set up.

"She must have called a press conference," Ayo says. "That's not good."

"I know. It means the cops don't have any clues."

"She's doing a callout for people to come forward." He glances at me, then goes back to watching Ella's mom. "You should be out there."

"Me? Why?"

"You were the last one to see Ella."

"I don't know," I say.

"Do you want me to come with you? I'll stand beside you."

We watch as Loni steps forward to the microphone the reporters have set up. We can't hear what she's saying, but she is standing very upright. Several times she turns away from the cameras to wipe her eyes.

"She's one tough lady. What did Ella call her?"

"The iron butterfly."

"Yeah, that's it. She'll be—" He stops. His eyes go wide as Loni's legs buckle. Suddenly she's a crumpled pile of clothing and tears. The reporters keep filming.

Mr. Wexford helps her up. He moves her to the side and then takes control of the mic. I still can't hear what anyone's saying, but I can guess.

Ella Larson was a straight-A student, and a wonderful and shining light at Fairmont High School. She has a bright future ahead of her. Her family and friends miss her. They want her back. If you have any information that could help, please phone.

He leads Ella's mom away. I want to chase after them. I want to tell them and the cops about my dad and Ella. There's no way—no way!—my dad would have done anything bad to Ella. But if that's true, why won't he say anything to Detective Tyron?

The bell rings. Ayo and I head to class, but I can't get the image of Loni sobbing out of my head. I've got to try again to talk to my dad. This time I'm going to push until I get some real answers.

Chapter Three

After school I find Dad in his office, laughing at his phone.

"What's so funny?"

His gaze flicks my way, and he quickly slides the phone into his pocket. "Oh, just a staff joke making the rounds." He seems a bit nervous. "Ready to go?"

I close the door. "I have to talk to you first."

A muscle twitches at the base of his jaw, and he forces a too-bright smile. "Whoa, this sounds serious. Hope I'm not going to be grounded."

"It's not a joke, Dad."

"Now I'm really worried about being grounded."

I take a breath and try to control my temper. And my fear. "It's about Ella—"

"Not this again." He shoves a pile of papers into his leather bag and slings it over his shoulder.

"I have to ask you—"

"No, no more asking, no more talking, no more. I'm sorry Ella's not talking to you or her mom. She's a good kid, but—"

"That's it? That's all you can say? Ella practically lived at our house for the past couple of years. She's almost family."

"But she's also an adult," says Dad. "Maybe we don't understand what she's doing. Maybe we don't agree with it, but those are Ella's decisions. She's a smart person, and she's responsible. If she took off, she must have her reasons for not telling anyone."

"How do you know?" I ask. "How do you know she wasn't upset and then someone took advantage of her?"

"Because Ella has a strong sense of survival," he says. "No matter what Loni says, that girl knows how to take care of herself. Trust me."

What is he hiding? "Fine, she's mad at her mom. Why would she freeze me out?"

"You know the answer to that—"

"She wouldn't do that! Ella wouldn't ignore me just because we had a fight. We've had lots of arguments."

"Maybe this was one fight too many."

"It's not like her!"

My dad sighs. "There's a point when people get tired of arguing. They get tired of feeling like they're not being heard. Ella was going through a rough patch at university. Her mom wasn't helping, and you weren't listening."

"Were you?"

"Yes. I told her to take a breath and do what she needed for self-care."

"So she took off and iced everyone out."

"I didn't say she did the mature thing," he says. "Look, I know you want to go into law enforcement, but you're not a detective just yet. Concentrate on your schoolwork, and let the cops do their job. If something happened to Ella, they'll find out. They'll get the answers."

This is my chance to make him tell me about that day. But I can't get the words out. My life is all about respecting my elders and not questioning my parents. It's the West Indian way. I'm trying to force myself to say what's necessary, but the only words I can find are, "But we—you—have information on Ella. You should talk to them."

"I did," he says. "The detective called me this morning, and I told him what I knew."

"What was that?"

"The last time I talked to her was a week ago. She was freaking out over school. I told her to take a breath and do what was right for her."

"That's it?" *What about the mall?* I want to ask, but I can't get the words out.

"What else would I tell them?" Dad asks. "That Loni was overprotective? That Ella decided she'd had enough and blew up her life? That she's probably on a beach in Mexico right now?"

"Is she?"

"God, Zack, how am I supposed to know that?"

"Because, Dad,"—I blurt out the words before my fear can stop me—"I saw you at the mall."

"What?"

"The mall. The day Ella went missing. I saw you at the mall." I swallow, but I can't get my throat muscles to work properly. "I saw you with Ella."

The room is dead quiet.

Dad's looking at me intently. I feel like I haven't taken a breath in a million years.

Then suddenly he's laughing. "Oh, Champ. You poor kid—I shouldn't laugh…"

I don't know whether to be relieved or mad. "You think it's funny?"

That stops him. "No, I'm sorry, Zack." He puts his hand on my shoulder. "I shouldn't have laughed. That was wrong. I was just thinking about you and your love for crime dramas.

How you create issues where there aren't any."

"I don't understand. What are you talking about?"

But he's not paying attention to my words. He looks into my eyes, his hand still on my shoulder. He squeezes. "God, what you must have thought. You must have been losing your mind, wondering why I didn't say anything to the police." He smiles, but there's sadness in it. "You poor kid, thinking you had to be loyal to me. It must have felt like you were betraying Ella."

"Yeah." The air rushes into my lungs. "That was exactly what it was like."

"You could have saved yourself a lot of pain if you'd come to me sooner."

"Yeah?"

"Yeah." He releases his grip and heads to the door. "I don't know what you think you saw, but it wasn't me and Ella. Like I told Detective Tyron, the last time I saw Ella was before she left for university."

My insides turn to ice. "What?"

"I wasn't at the mall. Maybe you saw Ella there, but I highly doubt it. You must have seen two people who looked like us. With all that's been going on, you thought you saw something you didn't."

"Dad—"

"I wasn't there, Champ." He looks at me hard. "If you tell the police otherwise, not only are you lying, but you're also leading them down the wrong path. They're going to waste time and resources chasing down a clue that only exists in your head."

"I know what I saw."

"I believe you," he says. "I believe you *think* you saw us. But you didn't."

He sighs. "Seriously. In a million years, do you think I'd ever hurt Ella?"

"No."

"If I had information that could help the police find her, don't you think I'd share it?"

"Yes."

"So why are we having this conversation? I wasn't at the mall with her, and you know I would help her if I could." He strides to the door and opens it. "So are we good to go?"

I take a second, then say, "Yeah, sorry, Dad. I must have been confused."

"It happens. I know you love your shows and the discovery of the eyewitness at the last second. But that stuff's fiction. In real life people mix up details all the time."

I nod, pretending I agree. But here's the thing. Eyewitness testimonies can be unreliable because it's a stranger looking at a stranger. I've lived with my dad all my life. I know what he looks like. I know his movements. And now I know something else. He's lying to me. Which means he *was* with Ella and she *did* get into his car. What I don't know is *why*. Why were they together? Why is my dad lying? And why did he just warn me off going to the police?

Chapter Four

The next day Dad tells me I have to take the bus home because he's got a meeting at another school. "Another one?" I say. "That's the second one this week."

"Professional development with the other guidance counselors," he says. "Best practices, new methods, all that crap. I don't know why it matters. To be good at this job, you only have to do one thing. Listen to kids when they talk."

"Which school?" The questions are out before I can stop myself. "How long will you be?"

"Why?" He grins. "Are you going to make sure I don't cut class?"

I force a laugh. "Yeah, I'll be checking your homework, young man."

"I'm scared." He fishes in his pockets and pulls out a twenty-dollar bill. "Here, grab a coffee on me for the ride home. I'll see you at dinner, Champ."

But he texts Mom around six and says the meeting's running late. She and I eat dinner by ourselves.

"I guess there must be a lot for those counselors to talk about," I say.

She doesn't answer. She just keeps pushing her carrots around the plate.

"Have you talked to Loni lately?" I ask. "Mom? *Mom*." She's completely zoned out.

"Sorry, honey." She looks up from her plate. "What did you say?"

"Ella's mom. Have you talked to her?"

Her fork falls to her plate. "What a mess," she says. "I hope this is just Ella being rebellious. That nothing serious has happened to her. Do me a favor. Never get into a car with someone you don't know. And don't talk to people you don't know. And if someone asks you to help them find a lost dog or cat—"

"Geez, Mom. I'm seventeen, not six."

"Elle is eighteen! And where is she?"

"I don't know."

We finish dinner in silence.

Dad comes home around eight. Mom's not happy.

"Why didn't you tell me you were going to be this late?"

"I texted you to eat without me, didn't I?" He throws his coat on a hanger and comes into the family room. "Hey, Champ."

"Because no school meeting lasts that long," says my mom, following him in. "Where were you really?" She is not letting this drop.

"God." He rolls his eyes and flops down in the armchair. "If you must know, *Mom…*"

The skin on her face tightens.

"Since I knew I was missing dinner, a bunch of us went out for wings and pizza afterward."

"And you couldn't bother letting me know? I made you dinner."

"There's this great invention," my dad says. "It's called a refrigerator? You put your food in it, and the next day you can reheat it. You should check it out. All the modern homes have them."

My mom snorts. "Modern? When's the last time we upgraded anything in this house? Everything's falling apart, and instead of taking care of things around here, you're out spending money partying with your friends."

Now it's my dad's face that gets tight. "Well, if it's money that's the problem, you'll be thrilled to know I'm selling the SUV."

"What?" I don't mean to get into their fight, but this is news.

They're too mad at each other to even notice I've said anything.

"Why are you selling it?" Mom perches on my armrest. She looks like an eagle about to swoop in for the kill.

"Because you're constantly on me about how much it's costing us." Dad reaches over and takes the remote. He goes to switch the channel, then notices it's already one with a game on. He tosses the controller back to me. "If I trade it in for something more economical, it'll save us money on monthly payments and gas. Besides, the SUV's a lemon. I always seem to be taking it into the shop for some stupid reason. The electronics don't work. The odometer is acting up. I had to take it in twice in the last three weeks."

Including the day Ella went missing. I remember him saying he had to go pick it up from the shop.

"Why did you finally decide to sell it now?" Mom's eyes narrow. "We've been talking about it for months."

"Because I'm sick and tired of your—" For the first time in this argument, he registers that I'm in the room. "Because it's good for the family." He stands. "I'm going to get something to eat."

"I thought you already ate." Mom shoots the words at his back.

"You made a big deal out of your fabulous homemade dinner, so I'm eating, okay?" He doesn't turn around.

Mom's on her feet in a flash and follows him into the kitchen.

I stay on the sofa. Maybe Dad's selling the SUV because he's tired of Mom harassing him about the money. But the timing's weird. I asked him about being with Ella at the mall, and now he's getting rid of the car?

Something's seriously wrong, and I have to figure out what it is.

Dad comes to my room a little later. "Sorry about earlier, Champ. It's not cool for your mom and I to fight in front of you."

"It's okay. Stuff happens, right?" I don't want him to stay, because I don't know what to say to him. On the other hand, I don't want him to leave, because I need him to tell me something that will stop the terrible thoughts in my head.

"How are you doing?"

"Fine," I say.

"You sure?" He comes over and sits on my bed. "You're not getting sick?"

"No. Why?"

His phone beeps. He pulls it out and checks the screen. Then he turns his attention back to me. "You had the game on. You *never* watch sports. What's going on?"

Man, he's better at catching clues than I am. "Nothing. You caught me in the middle of flipping channels."

"You sure?"

"What can I say? I was looking for something to watch when you came home. Then you and Mom…" I purposely trail off and look at him.

It's enough to make him stand. He rubs the back of his neck. "Yeah, I get it. Like I said, I'm sorry."

"Thanks."

"Sure." He heads for the door.

"Hey, Dad?"

"Yeah?"

"What was on your phone?"

"A very funny joke," he says, "but one for grown-ups only." He smiles. "I know you're almost an adult, but you know…" He points down the hallway. "I'm in enough trouble as it is. I don't need her yelling at me for corrupting you."

He gives me an easy smile, but I know he's hiding something. I'm tired of the lies, and I'm tired of asking him to be honest with me. If he won't give me the answers, I'll get them myself.

Chapter Five

Ayo drops into the seat across from me. We're at our favorite hangout, Al's Diner. We can't get enough of its greasy burgers and milkshakes so thick they can barely get up the straw.

"Oh, yeah, this is how you start a weekend." He scans the menu. "Fries and gravy it is. I am starving. What are you having?"

"I don't know yet."

"Seriously? You know the menu better than the servers do. What's up?" He tosses the menu onto the table. "You've been acting weird, which is saying a lot. You're weirdness personified. That means—"

"I know what *personified* means. My dad teaches English part time, remember?" The thought of my dad has the volcano in my stomach erupting.

"Whoa. Look at your face. Whatever it is, it's clearly about your folks." Ayo leans back. "They still fighting?"

"Yeah, but that's not it."

He waits.

"I don't know how to say it. You're going to think I'm crazy."

"Don't worry about that. I've known you since fourth grade." Ayo grins. "I *know* you're crazy. Talk."

"If you knew something, something that was important for other people to know, would you tell them?"

"Yes, of course. So tell me what's going on with you."

I fiddle with the cutlery on the table. Now that I have the chance, I realize how stupid and paranoid I'm going to sound.

"If you're waiting for me to read your mind, keep waiting. My superpowers are having incredible charm and getting out of Ms. Henderson's math class."

"It's my dad. He—he was with Ella the day she went missing."

"What?"

Just then the server comes to take our orders. As soon as she leaves, Ayo asks in a loud whisper, "What are you talking about?"

I tell him about seeing my dad at the mall with Ella. Ayo just nods, so I keep going.

"Later, when I was leaving the mall, I saw her get into our SUV."

"Mmm-hmm," says Ayo, his hand on his chin.

"Dad won't say anything to the detective. Says he wasn't at the mall. But now he's selling our car." I lean in close and drop my voice to an actual whisper. "Doesn't that seem suspicious?"

"Maybe, but maybe not." Ayo folds his hands on the table.

"What do you mean, *maybe*?"

"Zack, do you remember the time you thought you had meningitis?"

"I had a sore neck! That's one of the symptoms."

"Yes, but if you have meningitis, your neck is as stiff as a plank of wood. What you had was a bit of a stiff neck. Probably from sleeping on the bus."

I get where he's going with this. "You think I'm overreacting."

"Well, you do have a tendency to find conspiracies where there aren't any.

Especially since you decided you want to be a detective."

"Then why won't Dad tell the cops about his meeting with Ella?"

"Maybe that had nothing to do with her going missing," he says. "Your dad is one of the best guys I know. He wouldn't keep information from the cops if he thought it mattered."

"I guess, but it freaks me out that she's missing and my dad is obviously lying about what he knows."

"I don't blame you for freaking out," he says. "The whole thing is crazy. Loni is always losing her mind over every little thing. Ella can't sneeze without her mom shoving vitamin C pills down her throat and mainlining chicken soup into her veins."

"Still—"

Ayo smiles at the server as she sets down our drinks. After he takes a sip he says, "Listen, you're my bro, and overreacting or not, I've got your back. So take a breath and think this through. Really think about it."

"My dad was with Ella. She got into the car with him. Now Ella's missing. My dad's lying about seeing her." I raise my eyebrows in challenge.

"Okay, but let's play the other side. Loni has never allowed Ella to have a life. It's school, volunteer work and more school. Ella's never been to a party—she's never dated. Then she turns eighteen and goes to university miles away from her mother. Suddenly she can go where she wants, see who she wants." He takes another sip of his drink.

"Yeah, but—"

"But what? She's seeing the world. Her options are opening. I bet if her mom had let her travel like she said she wanted to instead of going to university, none of this would be happening."

"Okay, fine." I'm frustrated he won't come onside with me. It makes me wonder if this is how Ella felt when she told me she was thinking of quitting and I told her to stay in school. "Let's play your game. Ella has decided to run away and live a new life. Why hasn't she texted her mom?"

"Because she's pissed at her."

"Why didn't she text me?"

"You're one of her best friends. Instead of siding with her, you took her mom's side."

That hurts. "Of course I did. The first year at university is rough. Everyone knows that. She just needed a bit of extra time to settle in."

"Or maybe she realized she doesn't want to be a doctor and needed someone to hear her. And not even one of her best friends would listen."

"Okay, okay." I try to keep the irritation out of my voice. If this is how I made Ella feel, no wonder she was super mad at me. "So she's angry at me, her mom, the whole world. But the police are involved. If she's fine, why doesn't she tell them? Loni was on the news—"

"They were the *local* news stations. What if Ella's out of the country?"

"The police have no record of her booking a flight or catching a train."

"Are you sure?" he asks.

"No, but wouldn't that be one of the first things they'd check?"

"Good point. Say she took a bus to another city."

"But—"

"My point is, Ella could be quite far away. Maybe in some tiny town."

"And?"

"And unless she has access to Wi-Fi or the national news picks up her story, she may not even know any of this is going on. I've been checking her online feeds," he says. "She hasn't posted anything since she disappeared. Maybe she's still getting notifications, or maybe she's unplugged from everything because she doesn't want to deal. Think about it. You know Loni would be blowing up Ella's phone—texts, phone calls, app messages."

I scowl at him.

"What?"

"I hate it when you're logical."

Ayo grins. "Not just logical. I'm right." He leans back. "Go ahead, you can say it. *Ayo, you're right.*"

"You have a point, but we don't *know* if you're right."

"That was close," he says, "but you had too many words in there. Try again. *Ayo, you're right.*"

I toss the empty straw wrapper at him.

The server comes with our food. For a while there's no talking, only eating. Then we're back to talking about regular stuff—school, tests, his annoying little sister. But I still can't stop wondering about my dad.

Ayo can see it. He shoves his empty plate aside and says, "What's really going on?"

"Even if you've explained away the Ella thing—"

"With *logic*."

"Yeah, whatever. Something else is up with my dad. I feel it." I shake my head. "There's something else. Something in the air."

"I can tell you what's *not* in the air. Your dad being a criminal."

"Why wouldn't my dad say anything? If that's what it is, why wouldn't he just let Loni and the police know?"

"Maybe if he did, Ella would be in big trouble. I bet he's giving her time. That's your dad's way. He always gives people time to make the right decision."

"I guess, but holding back information is a crime."

"There has to be a reason," says Ayo. "Your dad wouldn't risk his job or his family over something stupid. He's not like that. I bet if she's not back in a couple of days, he'll say something."

"You really think she's okay? That she just took off?"

"I do. Trust me. With a thousand cousins, I grew up surrounded by drama. One of them was always taking off. They always came back."

"Yeah, but your family's wild."

He laughs. Then he says, "I don't blame you for worrying though."

"How do I stop?"

"You don't. Let's figure this out together. The cops are looking into Ella. How about if you and I figure out what's really going on with your dad? You said he's acting strange. Maybe it has to do with Ella. Maybe it's like your situation."

"Huh?"

"You have information, and you're not going to the detective, right? Maybe he's in the same boat."

"I never thought of that."

"There's a logical answer to all of this," he says. "You and me, we'll find out what it is."

Relief hits in a sudden rush. I don't have any answers, but at least now I have someone I can talk to, someone who'll help me figure it all out.

Chapter Six

We order dessert, and I go over everything I know. When I'm done, I sit back. "I know it sounds flimsy, but"—I hold up my hand when Ayo tries to interrupt— "lots of cases are solved with less."

"Real-life cases?"

"Maybe—yes! I can't think of any right now, but yes."

Ayo pulls some money out to pay for his meal. "Step one is easy. You think your dad gave Ella a ride somewhere, right?"

I nod.

"Cool. Let's check the vehicle's GPS history. It'll tell us where he's been."

"Man, that was so obvious. Why didn't I think of that?"

"Because you're smart, but you're not as smart as me."

"That's not true."

"And you overreact. A lot."

"I do not!"

He laughs. "They should have named you Chicken Little. You always think the sky's falling." He slides out of the booth.

"That's so not true." I follow him to the door.

"This from the guy who thought he saw a dead body on the way to school."

"It was foggy," I remind him, "and that bush looked like a person."

"Drama queen."

"Shut up."

We head back to my house. Both Mom and Dad are home. They're in the family room. Dad's reading, and Mom's working on a puzzle. For a second it stops me. It's been weeks since I've seen them do anything but glare at each other.

"Do you mind if I borrow the car?" I ask Dad.

"Where you going?" He drops his newspaper and gives Ayo a quick nod.

"The bluffs."

"Fill the gas tank?"

"Deal."

"We're out of bread," says Mom. "Can you get some while you're out? Grab some milk too."

"Double deal."

"You need to be back in two hours," she continues. "I have an alumni meeting."

Mom's keys are in the bowl on the table. Instead of taking them, I go to Dad's messenger bag and hunt through his stuff. If he asks, I'll say I was looking for his keys.

I root around but don't find much. Some pens from the hotels he stays at when he's at his conferences and a sandwich bag with a toothbrush and toothpaste. Nothing incriminating. No notes from Ella, no evidence I can overanalyze. I can hear Ayo mocking me.

I tell Ayo what I found—or didn't find—as we head to the garage. He climbs into the passenger seat while I open the garage door. Then I get inside the SUV and check the interior. "He cleaned the car."

"Don't freak out, bro. He's selling it. Of course he'd have it cleaned."

Once we're a couple of blocks from the house, I pull over. When I open the GPS history, all I get is an empty screen.

"He cleared out the locations too." I look at Ayo. "What does *that* have to do with selling the car?"

"It's a risky thing, selling the car directly. There can be a lot of crazies out there. Clearing the history just makes good sense. You want a total stranger knowing where you live, your regular routine?"

"Why do you always have an answer to everything?"

"Because you never have an answer to anything." He grins.

"You're hilarious."

"Listen," says Ayo. "You wanted to check into what your dad was doing because you think he's got information on Ella. So far, you haven't found anything."

"A lack of evidence doesn't mean a lack of—" I don't know how to finish the sentence in a clever way. "Still, something might have happened."

"You said Ella was back in contact with her dad, right?"

"Right, but I don't know anything about him. Besides, Detective Tyron is looking into that."

"Okay, so he's got that handled. And now that we've seen your dad doesn't have any secrets—"

"We don't know that, not for sure. There might be something on his phone." I check over my shoulder and then pull into the traffic.

"Good luck getting his phone. Good luck getting *anyone's* phone."

"I know. It's glued to his hand. I'm going to check his office first. I'll try to sneak a peek at his phone when he's sleeping. I bet his code is my birthday or something easy like that."

Ayo casts me a worried glance. "I'm not sure you should do that. Not unless we have actual proof your dad and Ella's disappearance are connected."

"Why? If it will help—"

"Your dad's a guidance counselor," he says. "There's confidential stuff on his phone. Emails, documents."

"So? I'm not looking for dirt on the kids he sees."

"Confidentiality rules are fierce. He could get in real trouble." He taps my hand. "Listen, man, I know we're playing detective, and I know you're worried about Ella. But you have to think about your dad too."

"I am. That's why I haven't gone to the police. If I'm wrong, it could cost my dad big-time. What if the police decide he's a person of interest? That's questioning and rumors. It will ruin his job."

"The same thing will happen if you start messing around in his office and phone. It's a breach of confidentiality. It could cost him his job—or worse."

"I wouldn't tell—"

"The truth will out, Zack. My grandma always says that. And she's right. It always does."

"Then how am I supposed to get the information?"

"I don't know, but you're the one who wants to be a cop. Police officers have to do things by the book. So do you."

"I'm not a cop yet."

"Consider it practice—"

"Ayo—"

"No." He shakes his head. "No way, Zack. When my family immigrated here, it wasn't easy. Seeing a therapist saved me, okay? She helped me figure out the mess in my head. It was a big deal, being able to talk to someone and knowing they'd keep my secrets. I won't let you violate someone's privacy. You do that, and I'm out—out of your crazy hunt, and out of our friendship too."

I believe he means it. But I'm stuck in this weird triangle. Ayo on one side, my dad on another, and Ella on the last. Out of all of them, Ella's the priority. She's the one who might be in physical danger. Still, maybe I don't need to go through Dad's phone just yet. This isn't a fight I'm willing to have with Ayo. At least, not right now. "Okay. I'll leave the phone out of it," I say.

"Good. Let's focus on Ella's dad."

"We should head home and check Ella's online stuff," I say. "If her dad was kicking around, he might have commented on one of her posts."

"Fair, but we can't go back yet. We told your folks we'd be at the bluffs. It's going to look weird if we suddenly come back. Besides, we can check her stuff right now on our phones."

"I know, but Mom has cook-up rice at home."

"With beef and hot peppers?"

I nod.

Ayo squints at the cloudless sky. "Hmm. Looks like rain. We should head back."

We stop at the grocery store and pick up the bread and milk. I fill up the tank with gas.

"Back so soon?" Dad asks as we walk in. He grins and fist-bumps Ayo.

"Thought it might rain," I say. "Where's Mom?"

"On the phone with Loni."

Ayo and I lock eyes.

"Why?" Ayo asks. "What happened?"

Dad shrugs. "I don't know. The phone rang. Your mom picked it up. Then she went to the bedroom and closed the door."

"I'll put the bread and milk away," says Ayo. "Why don't you see if you can find out what's going on."

I head down the hallway. I tap softly on the door, then step into the room.

Mom's sitting on the bed. She spots me and holds up her hand. "Okay, okay. No, I'll talk to Zack when he gets home." She listens, talks for a few more seconds, then hangs up. "Good timing."

"What's going on?"

"You ever heard of a kid named Gavin?"

"No. Who is he?"

"Believe it or not, he was Ella's boyfriend."

"Ella had a boyfriend?" The question comes out louder than I meant it to.

"Ella had a *what*?" Ayo's question rings out from down the hall.

Mom moves past me and heads back toward the kitchen.

I chase after her. "It can't be—she would've told me. She tells me everything."

"Did you know that Ella had a boyfriend?" she asks Ayo.

"No! I didn't think Ella liked anyone," he says.

"Well, apparently she did." Mom sits down at the table. "It wasn't a long-term thing, but she and this guy were dating." She makes a face. "It didn't end well."

"How do you know?" I ask.

"Loni said the police talked to Ella's dorm roommate but suspected the girl wasn't telling them everything. Turns out she wasn't upfront about Gavin because she liked him too."

The questions crowd my brain. I can't think of which one to ask first. "What?"

"Gavin, Ella and the roommate met in statistics class. Both girls were interested in him, but he preferred Ella. They dated for a bit. But Ella broke it off after a few weeks. The guy started texting her, leaving presents, following her around on campus." Mom looks disgusted. "The roommate thought Gavin was being romantic."

"Sounds more like stalking to me," says Ayo.

"Me too," I add.

"Me three," says Mom. "The police tracked Gavin down and have been questioning him. So Loni was filling me in." She glances at her watch. "I've got to get ready. I told Loni I'd try and stop by before my meeting." She gets up and plants a kiss on my cheek. "Dinner's in the microwave."

"We should definitely check Ella's feeds," says Ayo after Mom is out of earshot.

I agree, but I'm still in shock about not knowing Ella had a boyfriend. I'm even more upset that she never told me about him giving her a hard time.

"Did Ella ever talk to you about the guy?" Ayo asks as we load up our plates.

"No." There's a weird churning in my stomach. Not fear. Not nerves. It's something else. Ella was keeping secrets. If that's true, then maybe Ayo is right. Maybe she did take off and doesn't care who's worried about her. But it doesn't mesh with the Ella I knew. That's what's making my stomach hurt. I'm starting to wonder how well I knew her. I'm starting to wonder if I even knew her at all.

Chapter Seven

"So Ella had secrets. Who doesn't?"
Ayo says when we're safely in my room
and I tell him what I'm thinking.

"I don't."

"Right. You think your dad has
information on Ella."

"That's *his* secret."

"And you're keeping it," says Ayo.
He points at me. "That's *your* secret."

"Can you blame me?" I show him my phone. "Since we learned about this Gavin guy, look at what's going on online. Everyone's talking about it, about him."

Ayo takes the phone and scrolls through the feeds. "Oh, man."

"Yeah, it's creepy. All it took was one post from Ella's mom about him. Suddenly everyone's got an opinion. Can you imagine what would happen if I outed my dad? It would ruin everything."

"Hey, I'm not judging," says Ayo. "If it was my dad, I probably wouldn't say anything either." He stands. "I should head home. We should talk to Loni tomorrow."

"About what?"

"Ella's dad. You said Ella had reconnected with him, right? Loni's got to have information about her ex."

"I don't know. From everything I've heard, their divorce was nuclear war."

"Exactly," says Ayo. "So she'll be able to help. If my aunts and uncles have taught me anything, it's that adults love talking about their terrible exes."

A sound wakes me up in the middle of the night. I hear muffled voices. Then the thump of something hitting the floor. I get out of bed and stand at the top of the dark stairs. I can see Mom at the bottom. A lamp from the living room is the only light. She's bent over a garbage bag, shoving something inside. It takes me a second to realize it's Dad's clothes. On top is his favorite wool coat. The one he was wearing the day I saw him with Ella. I creep away from the steps and sneak back to my room.

When Ayo picks me up the next morning I don't tell him about what I saw. Even for me it feels way over the top to think my whole family is involved in a grand conspiracy with Ella. Still, Mom shoving all Dad's stuff in a bag says that whatever's going on between them is getting worse.

Ayo drives us to Ella's house. As we pull into the driveway, I realize how awful all of this must be for her mom. I should have been there for her. And that makes me angry at my dad. Angry that my loyalty to him has kept me away.

Ella's mom takes a while to answer the door. When she finally opens it, it's obvious she hasn't slept in days. She blinks as though trying to remember who we are. "Zack? Ayo? What are you doing here?" She reaches out to us. "Did you hear something from Ella? Did she call you?"

"No, I'm sorry," I say. "We haven't heard from her. But we wanted to see how you were doing."

"Oh." Her voice goes flat. "I'm good. Thank you, boys." She starts to close the door.

"Wait, Loni. Can we come in? Can we talk?"

She brushes her hair back. "Yes, sure." She steps aside to let us in. "I'm afraid I don't have much to offer you. I haven't had time to—"

"It's fine." Ayo holds up a bag of bagels and a tray of coffees. "We brought supplies. We thought you might be hungry."

"That's very sweet of you." She moves down the hallway. "But I'm afraid I don't have much of an appetite these days."

Ayo and I look at each other. We had hoped to get Ella's mom to relax over some food and coffee. Then we could ask her about her husband. Now it feels like a jerk move.

"So, how can I help you?" She sits down on the living-room couch.

"Just wanted to make sure you were eating," said Ayo, "and—uh—sleeping okay."

"You can see I'm doing fine, under the circumstances."

"Right." I wipe my hands on my jeans. "The cops, have they updated you on the case?"

"Not really," she says with a frown. "Even this Gavin kid, the police won't tell me what they learned." She leans forward. "That boy was harassing her. He spread terrible rumors about my daughter, but you know what those officers did? They let him go. They let him go! They said they didn't have enough evidence, said he wasn't in town the day Ella went missing. But that stuff can be faked, right?" Her eyes are wide, angry. "He could be phishing or twerking or whatever it is they do these days."

Normally, an adult mixing up tech and dance terms would be hilarious. But there's nothing funny about Loni's rage.

"I watch TV. I know you can fake an alibi. How do we know this boy didn't do that? I asked the police to let me talk to him—begged to talk to him." She puts her face in her hands. "But they won't let me. They say it's not appropriate."

"Did they say anything else?" I ask.

"Like what?"

I clear my throat. "Maybe about your ex-husband?"

Ella's mom goes still. "What about him?"

"Did the cops tell you that Ella had reconnected—"

She waves me off. "I heard. It's not true. My ex owes me thousands of dollars, tens of thousands, in child support. If he had contacted Ella, she would have told me, and I would have had the lawyers on him. He knows that. Phil would never have talked to Ella."

"Ella said—"

"It must have been someone else," she says. Her hands flutter in agitation. "Someone who pretended to be him. Ella was trusting and easily manipulated—"

"She knows her dad."

"Maybe when she was a child." Loni spits out the words. "But it's been years, and her loyalty is to me."

"Maybe that's why she didn't tell you," Ayo says gently. "Maybe she was worried about hurting you—"

"She never went near that man. That would have been a betrayal of everything I've done for her. She wouldn't do that!" She rose to her feet. "I think it's time for you boys to leave."

"We didn't mean to upset you," I say quickly.

"Ella and I have had to survive together. We're a team, best friends. I know everything about my daughter. We don't have secrets."

I don't know what to say.

Ayo's expression mirrors what I'm feeling. Horror at watching Ella's mom unspool, frustrated because there's nothing we can do to make it better. She's shrieking now, yelling about all the ways she and Ella are united. Screaming that if people would just listen to her, they'd find her daughter. "We can be a family again," she says and then collapses back on the couch.

The silence is a relief.

"Loni—" I begin.

"Get out," she says, her voice barely a whisper now. "I'm fine. Get out."

"Well, that didn't go the way I expected," I say to Ayo as we walk down the front steps to the car. "I shouldn't have come here. I shouldn't have brought up her ex-husband."

"Life's about asking hard questions and being cool when people get mad at you. But that was intense. Poor Mrs. Loni." Ayo climbs in and puts on his seat belt. "At least we found out something. Two somethings, if you think about it." He starts the car.

"What's that?" I buckle in.

"She and Ella aren't as close as she thinks."

"We knew that."

"No, we knew there was stuff between them because of Ella. Now we know Mom thinks her kid didn't keep any secrets from her."

I don't really get his point, but I nod. "And the second thing?"

"Something happened the day Ella went missing. Something her mom doesn't want us to know."

I think about that for a moment. "Assuming Ella wasn't kidnapped, assuming she's taken off, it makes sense. Profilers always talk about a trigger, something that happens that makes the person in question snap." I think about it some more. "But moms and daughters fight all the time, so it couldn't have been something regular."

"Or maybe it was the straw that broke the camel's back. Maybe it was one fight too many."

That's similar to something Dad said too. I'd been hoping the visit with Ella's mom would clear up things. Instead, all I have are more questions and more secrets to untangle. What I do know is that I am tired. Tired of not knowing where Ella might be. Tired of watching Loni come apart every time her daughter's name is mentioned. Most of all, I'm tired of not knowing what part my dad has played in all of it. I may not have the answers, but I know what I'm going to do next. I'm going to find my dad and force him to tell me the truth about what happened that day at the mall.

Chapter Eight

"When is Dad going to be back?" I ask Mom as soon as I get home.

She shrugs. "How am I supposed to know?"

"You're his wife—"

She snorts. "You're his son. Why don't *you* know where he is?"

"Jeez, Mom. I was just asking."

Mom is on the couch, flipping through the channels. "Why don't you phone him? Leave me out of it."

"I tried. But it went to voice mail."

"Did you leave a message?"

"Yeah."

More channel flipping. "Well then, I'm sure he'll get back to you soon."

"Can you cut the attitude?" That's usually Mom's line. I can't believe I just said it to her! "I mean, I don't know what's going on between the two of you—"

"Nothing. There's nothing going on—"

"You know, my friend's missing. I'm trying to talk to Dad, and he's not around. And you're not even paying attention—"

Mom shuts off the TV, stands and turns to me. It's a solid, fluid motion, and it catches me off guard. "Well, we all have people who are missing. As a matter of fact, I have a missing husband."

"Yeah—"

"He's been missing for weeks, because even when he's here, he's not here."

"Is that why you threw out his clothes?"

"What?"

"The other night, I saw you throw away his favorite jacket."

"You saw that?"

"He's going to be pissed."

She smirks.

She's happy. I'm freaking out, and she thinks this is some kind of party. I have had it with both of them.

"You think this is funny?" I yell. "Dad's keeping secrets—I saw him at the mall with Ella." It slips out before I can stop myself, but I'm too mad to care.

"Now he's suddenly selling the car, and you're throwing out the jacket he wore that day—"

She freezes. "Wait a minute. You think your dad's involved in Ella's disappearance?"

"What else could it be?"

Mom doesn't say anything for a moment. "Your dad doesn't have anything to do with Ella going missing."

"But he's acting weird. Why?"

Silence.

I stare at her, rearranging everything I know. Instead of bringing Ella into it, I go over each piece of information by itself. Mom and Dad fighting. The money troubles. Dad working late. The way he's glued to his phone. The messages that come through.

"He's having an affair, isn't he?"

She still won't say anything. The way the tears fall, though, tells me everything.

I'm such an idiot. I want to be a detective and solve crimes. But I couldn't even see what was right in front of me all along.

She points to the chair. Dad's briefcase is on it. "He says he's at a meeting, but he left all his work stuff here. He's given up pretending. I'm sorry, Zack."

I grab his briefcase and go to my room. I want to fling it at the wall. I want to break holes in the drywall and smash my fists into the furniture. But then I realize something. I don't want to destroy my bedroom. I want to punch my dad.

I drop the briefcase on the floor and dump out its contents. There's nothing in it that can tell me where he might be. It's a bunch of stupid hotel pens and—wait. I look at each of the pens. They're all local hotels.

All the times he told us he was at a meeting or at a conference, he was still here. He was staying at a hotel with someone else. All the lies. All the stupid smiles, calling me "Champ," pretending he still cared about the family. I go back out to talk to my mom.

She's crying, and her face is red. "I'm sorry," she says. "About everything."

"Me too." My voice is flat. "Where is Dad?"

"Honey, I don't think—"

"He has information about Ella. I need to talk to him. Where is he?"

Eventually she gives me an address. It's for the other woman's house. "Her name's Jenny."

I text Ayo and tell him what's going on.

I don't know what to say. He replies immediately.

> *The stuff between Mom and Dad can wait. I want answers about Ella.*

That's a bad idea, dude.

> *Either you drive me, or I take a cab. Your choice.*

Okay, I'm coming.

When Ayo arrives, I hand him the paper. "Here's the address," I say. "Let's go."

"In a minute," he says. "First I need you to calm down."

"I am calm."

"Zack, I'm not playing. I only came here because I'm worried you're going to do something stupid."

My hand reaches for the car door, but Ayo starts driving.

"You're under a lot of stress, and you've had a couple of bad things happen. Ella's missing. Your dad's… gone."

"He's not gone. He's off with some chick. He should be at home. Helping me deal with my missing friend. But he isn't. He's off with *Jenny*—"

"Right, and now you want to go and yell at him. I get that. Actually, I'm all for you screaming at him. I need to make sure that's all you're going to do."

"I can't promise I won't punch him."

Ayo sighs. "Let's go somewhere else, at least until you calm down."

"We go to Jenny's house. You take me anywhere else, and I'm taking a cab."

He shakes his head, but he turns down the street, and heads to her place.

Chapter Nine

Ayo parks in front of Jenny's house.
I don't know what I expected. Maybe
a house with peeling paint and broken
windows. Instead, her house is pretty.
White with blue trim, flower boxes and
a green lawn.

"You okay?"

"No." I climb out of the car. Behind
me I hear the other car door slam shut.

"I should do this alone." I don't bother turning around.

Ayo jogs up beside me. "Yeah, like I'm going to leave you alone."

I get to the front door and lift my hand to ring the bell.

"Are you sure you want to do it like this?" Ayo asks softly.

I ring the bell. By the time the door opens, anger, fear and pain are rushing through my body.

A woman I assume is Jenny smiles. Her gaze goes from Ayo to me. "Yes?"

"I'm Zack. I'm looking for my father."

Her smile is uncertain. "I think you have the wrong house—"

"Patrick Bernard. He's here when he should be at home with me and my mom."

The blood rushes from her face.

"My mom said I could find him here. I need to talk to him about one of my friends. She's missing. She was with him the day she went missing, but he's lying about it. That shouldn't be a surprise to any of us, though, right? We all know he's a liar."

Jenny tries to close the door, but I block it with my foot. "Is he here?"

"N-no." She forces a smile. "Patrick and I are just friends. I don't know what you and your mom are thinking."

"We're thinking my dad's a slime-ball. I don't know what she thinks of you, but I think—"

"He's at the gym." The words come out in a rush, and then she slams the door in my face.

Ayo puts his hand on my arm and pushes me down the stairs.

I catch Jenny watching from her windows and give her the middle finger.

She ducks her head and moves away.

"Trust him to screw around with a coward," I mutter. "The least she could do is face the consequences."

"Speaking of consequences, we're attracting a crowd," says Ayo. A couple of people are out on their lawns, pretending to do yard work.

"Good. They should know what kind of neighbor they have."

He shoves me toward the car. "Your fight is with your dad."

I try to step away, but he grabs me and marches me down the sidewalk.

"Fine," I say. "You want me to deal with him. I'm good with that. She said he was at the gym. I know which one he uses. Let's go. I can talk to him about Ella *and* his new little friend."

Ayo shakes his head. "You're in a bad way. Let's go home."

"I want answers."

"I do too, but now isn't a good time."

"Good old Ayo. Always the smart one. Always so calm."

"Not always, but in this case, one of us needs to be."

"In this case, there only needs to be one of us," I say. "I'm going to the gym."

"It's not a good idea."

"The whole reason we came here is to find out what my dad knows about Ella. So that's what I'm going to do."

"No, you're not. You're not making any sense. First, you're mad at this woman, then you want to talk to your dad, then you want to—"

"I didn't ask for your opinion. In fact, I don't want you near me."

"Zack—"

"Go back home," I tell him. "Go back to your perfect family."

"My family's not—"

I shove him aside and head down the sidewalk. I don't care what he says, and

I don't care what he thinks. I'm going to keep my cool and talk to my dad. My priority is Ella. I'll figure out the rest of it later.

Chapter Ten

When I get to the gym, there's no one at the reception desk. Which is fine, but to get into the members' section and the workout area, you need a card. Luckily, it's lunchtime, and everyone's coming and going.

A lady uses her card, and I catch the door as she walks in. She looks back at me.

I smile. "Looking for my dad, Patrick Bernard."

She smiles back. "Oh, yes. I know him."

I bet every woman at the gym knows him. It takes some walking around, but I find him at the free weights. He's covered in sweat. "Zack?" He sets down the set of dumbbells. "What are you doing here?"

"I want answers."

"What?" He looks at me like I've lost my mind. Then he glances around and sees the other gym goers watching.

"I want to talk about Ella—"

"Oh, for God's sake." He's annoyed. "There's nothing wrong with Ella."

"I saw you with her," I say. "I saw you with her the day she disappeared."

No one's moving. They're staring at Dad.

"I don't know what you think you saw, but—"

"Stop it! Stop lying to me. I know what I saw, just like I know about your *girlfriend*."

Dad freezes. "You know about Jenny?"

"Mom gave me her address."

"Your *mom* knows?" He looks like he's going to throw up. "Listen, Zack, I know what you're thinking, but let me explain—"

"I don't care about any of it," I say. It's a lie, but who cares? If he can be a liar, why can't I? "I want to know about Ella."

He goes to put his hand on my shoulder, but I swing aside. His hand is frozen in midair. "Let's go to the change-room, okay? We can talk there."

I follow him in silence. There's a couple of guys in the room, so Dad takes us to a deserted corner. "About that day," he starts.

"No more lies."

He holds up his hands. "No more lies." Dad takes a breath. "I did see Ella."

The rush of validation whooshes through me. It's quickly burned up by the anger that follows. "I knew it! This whole time I kept asking, and you kept lying!"

"You can scream at me," he says quietly, "or you can listen."

"You lied to me. You made me question my own eyes."

Dad says, "I know you're angry, and I deserve it. But let me talk, okay?"

I swallow the words and the rage. "Fine."

He sits next to me. His Adam's apple bobs up and down. "I met Jenny at a conference a few months ago."

I'm tempted to interrupt, but I keep my mouth shut.

"Your mom and I—" He licks his lips. "It hasn't been good for a while."

"But it hadn't been bad," I say dully. "I lived with you, remember?"

For a second I think he's going to cry. "Marriage shouldn't be about surviving because things aren't too bad. There's stuff you didn't see, things you don't know."

"Like what?"

He shakes his head. "I don't want to get into it."

"But cheating with Jenny? That was your solution?"

He winces. "No—I—let me finish." He takes a breath. "Jenny and I...it just sort of happened. We've been seeing each other for a while now. I thought your mom suspected. I wasn't sure, but—"

"She's not stupid."

He goes back to looking like he's going to cry. "No, she's not."

"What does any of this have to do with Ella?"

"Ella saw us, Jenny and me. She was angry, said that I had betrayed everyone." Before I can respond, he says, "Ella demanded that I come clean. She wanted me to tell you and your mom about Jenny."

My skin goes cold.

"The day at the mall, Ella and I met. She said I had until the end of the day or she was going to tell you." He glances at me. "She was devastated. Ella's not my kid, but she has spent a lot of time at our house over the years. All I could think was that if she was this devastated, what would the news do to you?" He shakes his head. "I told her I was going to tell you, but I lied. I just couldn't." He slumps and passes his hand over his eyes. "I lied about everything. I'm sorry, Zack—"

"Get back to Ella."

"There's nothing else. The next day, when you didn't come flying at me, I figured she hadn't told you."

"But then she disappeared and cut off contact with everyone."

"I thought it was because of the affair. She couldn't tell you, but she didn't know how to keep it from you. So she took off so she had time to think."

"And didn't tell anyone?"

He shifts and looks away.

"Is that why you didn't care when she disappeared?"

"I do care, but—"

"But what? You don't know if Ella's okay, but you didn't care because it kept your secret safe," I say. "All your stupid talk about her needing space and having reasons for doing stuff that we don't understand. It was never about her—it was about you."

"Zack—"

"What happened after your talk?"

"I met Jenny at the movie theater. We watched a show, then…" He swallows. "We went to her place."

"But Ella, where did you take Ella?"

He frowns. "What do you mean? I didn't take Ella anywhere."

"I saw the two of you get into our car."

"The day she disappeared? That's impossible. The car was in the shop. It was there all day."

"But you said you had to go pick it up."

His face goes red. "When I left that day, it wasn't to get the car. I was at Jenny's house. I used her car to go meet Ella. I didn't get our SUV until later that night."

"But I saw you in the parking lot."

"Me? You actually saw me?"

I think back. "No, but it was our car and Ella. Same make, same model—"

"It might have been the same make and model, but we're not the only family with that vehicle."

"It had the zombie decals on it."

"Are you positive?" He puts his hand on my shoulder.

I shrug it off. "I'm positive. It was our decals on the back windshield. I know it."

"You have to believe me, Zack. I didn't do anything other than see Ella at the mall. I didn't tell the cops because they would have asked why we were meeting. I didn't want you to know about Jenny. I wasn't driving the car—but this could be a clue. I'll tell the police everything, I promise."

I'm barely listening. If Dad's not lying this time, then someone used our car. I play back all the information I know and try to rearrange it in a way that makes sense. How could it have been our SUV if it was in the shop? And Dad picked it up that night!

I've got it. "Ella's mom works for the dealership. What if she was the one who picked up Ella?"

Dad frowns. "Loni? Why would she take our car? She's got her own vehicle."

"Because she didn't want anyone to know what she was doing."

"Son, Loni did not steal our car—"

But I'm already out the door.

Chapter Eleven

Ayo's standing in front of the gym entrance. "Glad to see you didn't do anything that would have gotten you arrested."

"How do you know they didn't call the cops?"

"Because you're not in handcuffs."

"Listen, about what happened—"

"We'll talk later. You have enough drama going on right now."

"Great, because I have a new theory."

"Oh god."

"No, listen." I tell him about Dad and my new suspect.

Ayo's eyes bug out. "Are you insane? I mean it. Have you lost what little sense you had?"

"Think about it. Ella's always been under her mom's thumb. Then she gets into university and starts finding freedom. But her mom won't let up, and Ella's fighting back."

"So Loni steals your car, takes her daughter from the mall and is holding her hostage. At the same time, she's risking jail time by pulling the cops into a fake missing-person case."

"When you say it like that—"

"Like what? Like a sane person would say it?"

"At least let's talk to her," I say.

"No. No! The last time we did, she went to pieces, and I felt like a piece of crap for doing it to her."

"I'll talk to her. You can wait in the car."

Ayo looks at me hard. "Do you have any idea what a total lunatic you are?"

"Okay, fine, so it's not Ella's mom. But *someone* used our car."

"You were too far away to see the driver. That means you couldn't have seen the license plate."

"But I saw the zombie decals."

"Everybody has zombie decals! Do you not realize how insane this is? First, you think your dad is hiding information about Ella—"

"He was."

"No, he was hiding information about his affair," says Ayo. "But now that he's come clean with his information, you think it's her mom? It doesn't make sense."

"This is my last theory," I beg. "Give me this. If I'm wrong, I'll leave it alone. I promise."

"I doubt it."

"No, I swear on our friendship. If Loni doesn't know about the car, I'll leave it alone."

He gives me another hard stare. "I'm going with you, but not because I believe you. I'm going to make sure your harebrained theory doesn't hurt Ella's mom. You'll treat her with dignity and respect."

I hold out my hand. "Deal, but I'm right. In the majority of crimes, it's a loved one who is responsible."

He mutters something I can't hear, and then we climb into his car. Ayo starts the engine, and we head off to solve the mystery of Ella's disappearance.

Chapter Twelve

But Ayo doesn't go to Ella's house.

"Why are we back at my place?" I ask.

"Because you're a lunatic, and I'm not letting you bully that poor woman."

"I'm not going to bully her! I want some answers about what really happened between her and Ella."

"What happened? Zack, I love you like a brother, but don't be an idiot! She and Ella had a fight and Loni probably said something she can't take back. And now her daughter's missing—either because she took off, or because something terrible happened."

"Right, so we need to talk to her—"

Ayo smacks his fist against the steering wheel. "Stop it!"

"What is your problem?"

"What is yours? Think about it. The woman is drowing in guilt. And you want to accuse her of hurting her daughter?"

"Statistically—"

"This isn't statistics. It's not a weird lamp shadow on your wall or a tree stump in the fog. This is a real live person with real live feelings. Is that what you want to do to Ella's mom? Tell her you think she's capable of something like that?"

"No, but—"

"Then why are you doing this?"

"Because someone has to have the answers. Ella couldn't have just disappeared into thin air. Someone must have taken her."

"Why? Why can't it be that she took off—"

"How could she not tell me? If that's true—"

"Then she's a jerk. And maybe right now that's what she is. Sometimes when people are hurting, they say and do hurtful things," Ayo says.

"She should've trusted me. Because now I don't know if she's taken off somewhere, or if she's cold and scared…" My phone rings, and for a second I think it might be Ella. But it's Dad.

"Where are you?" he asks when I pick up.

"At the house."

"Ella's? I don't see your car."

"No, I'm home. Why are you at Ella's?"

"Because you acted like you were going to go to her house and accuse Loni of harming her child. Thank god you changed your mind. I'm heading to the police station to update my statement. Do you want to meet me? Maybe we can talk?"

"Yeah, sure," I say. I don't want to talk to him, but I want to make sure he tells the detective the truth.

"Great. I'll meet you there."

I end the call and turn to Ayo. "Dad's going to the cops to change his statement."

"I'm taking you there." He puts the car in gear. "Let the professionals handle you."

"Ayo—"

"Loni didn't hurt her kid."

"But—"

"Did you ever think that maybe you're overreacting about Ella because of your mom and dad?"

"What are you talking about?"

"Your parents are fighting, and you knew something was wrong between them. Then Ella starts acting weird and takes off."

"You think I've focused on Ella so I didn't have to think about my parents?"

"I think there are a lot of people letting you down right now, and you need to keep yourself together."

I look at him. "Not everyone though. You have my back."

"Just barely," he says. "Once this is figured out, we have to have a talk. I'm your friend, Zack. You don't get to treat me like crap because you're in a bad place."

"I'm sorry," I say, and I mean it. I don't want to do to him what Ella might be doing to me.

"I accept, but only because you're buying me lunch or dinner. Maybe both," he says. "At Al's Diner. You can tell me how it went with your dad."

Chapter Thirteen

I'm with Dad when he makes his statement to Detective Tyron.

Then it's my turn to tell the cop what I've been holding back. "I thought I saw Ella get into the SUV with my dad."

"It wasn't me," says Dad. "I was using...my girlfriend's car."

The detective takes down all the information, asks some questions.

Then he closes his notebook. "Do you two realize what you've done? Withholding information is a big deal."

"It wasn't Zack's fault," Dad says.

But the detective's not having any of it. "You want to be a police officer, Zack? To help people? Then it means you always do the right thing, even when it's not the easy thing."

"That's not fair," Dad says. "I'm his father."

The detective doesn't say anything. He stares at Dad until my dad looks away.

"I'm going to see what I can find out about this." Detective Tyron stands. "I'll also be following up with the both of you about your actions."

I want to ask him if he'll tell me what he finds out, but it's obvious he wants nothing more to do with either of us.

Dad and I leave the station. "Do you want to get something to eat?"

"Actually, I'd rather go home," I say. "I'm all talked out."

He nods, and we drive home in silence.

The next afternoon Dad calls me to his office.

"I got a phone call from the detective," he says. "You did see our car at the mall. Apparently, one of the mechanics at the shop has been using client cars for a side business in a ride share. He takes the cars for the test drive, picks up a fare. The guy is smart. Short trips. Then he claims some kind of extra trouble with the vehicle."

"So he picked up Ella?"

Dad nods. "So now the detective has a drop-off location for Ella, and he's going to follow up on it."

Ella, white-faced and shaking, is on my doorstep later that night. When she sees me, she starts crying and flings her arms around me. "Oh my god, Zack. I'm so sorry."

I'm angry and happy at the same time. "What happened? Where were you?"

"Zack, what's going on?" Mom comes around the corner, sees Ella and screams. She runs and pulls her into a hug.

"Are you okay? What happened?"

"I was with my dad at the cabin. I had no idea what was going on."

I can't understand the rest because she's crying so hard. Mom takes her into the kitchen.

"I'd been talking to my dad on and off lately," says Ella. "And I didn't have anyone to talk to about…all the stuff that's been going on." Her gaze slides from us, and I know she's including my dad in *stuff*.

"It's okay," Mom says. "We know about my husband's…extracurricular activities."

"I called my dad," she says, "and he said to come over. I used the Rider app to call a cab. The driver picked me up in your car." She shakes her head. "It was so stupid. As soon as I saw the car, I knew he wasn't supposed to be using the SUV. I smelled the grease on him. I figured he must be one of the mechanics from the dealership. But I was so mad at your dad, I thought, Screw it. If someone wanted to use his car, what did I care?"

Ella sniffs. "He dropped me at my dad's. Then Dad and I hung out for a bit. We went for a drive in the country. He showed me this old cabin that's been in his family for years. When I was really small, we used to go there for long weekends. Anyway, Dad said I could stay there for a bit."

"But you didn't have any clothes or food," says Mom.

"There was a small strip mall in the town. Dad bought everything I needed. When I got back to the cabin, I tried to text Mom, but there was no reception. Dad said he'd let Mom know." She starts crying again. "Dad came by a couple of times that week. He said he'd had this long talk with Mom, and she was cool about giving me some space. Then he said it was good that I was having a hard time because it had forced them to talk. I believed him, and I thought maybe he was right. Even though things were tough, maybe it was good if it meant having both my parents in my life."

Mom hands her a tissue.

"Thanks," she says. "It's such a mess. Dad knew about the investigation and didn't come forward to me or the cops.

He just wanted to get back at my mom. I think the cops are going to charge him with obstruction or misleading a police investigation or something."

Her words make me think of my dad. Ayo said my dad wouldn't do anything that risked his job or his family, but now he's done both. He kept information from the cops, which might mean a fine, prison time—even his job. And he cheated on my mom. Now Mom wants a divorce.

Then there's me. I kept information from Detective Tyron too. I'm not sure what that will mean. Will I be charged for obstruction? Have I blown my chance for a career in law enforcement?

Ella touches my hand, and it brings my focus back to the table.

"I wanted some space, that's all," she says. "A quiet place to think, and I thought I had it. And I thought my dad had changed, but he's as bad as my mom said. She's mad and disappointed, and I don't know what happens from here."

"It will take time," says Mom. "But you and Loni will get through this. I promise. I'm glad you're safe. I'm just so glad you're safe."

Ella squeezes my fingers. "Zack, I'm so sorry about all of this. The cops and my mom said you were trying to help, and I feel terrible. I didn't know about any of it until Detective Tyron showed up at the cabin." She rises from the chair. "I have to go. I promised my mom I wouldn't stay long. We have a lot to talk about." She looks at me. "But we should catch up soon, okay?"

I nod. I'm glad she's okay. But now that I know she's safe, I'm thinking about how she didn't tell me she was seeing her dad or about her ex-boyfriend. I'm still kind of mad she iced me out instead of talking to me or at least saying she needed some space. "Maybe in a couple of days. I need some time to think."

"Yeah, I get that." She smiles, but there are tears in her eyes. "I really am sorry, Zack. It was stupid to cut you off like that."

I don't want to say, *It's fine*, because it's not. Plus, it would be a lie, and I've had enough of people lying. I walk her to the door, and then I text Ayo and give him the whole story.

How do you feel?

Everything's a mess. I just want to run away from it all. Think Ella will tell me where the cabin is?

Not a good idea. There's no reception, right? How are you going to get your crime shows?

I've had enough of crime.

How about you buy me that burger you owe me instead?

"Mom, I'm going out with Ayo, okay?"

"You sure you don't want to stay home, maybe talk?" She comes up to me. "We have a lot to discuss."

"I know, but right now I need some space. We're going to grab some grub from Al's."

"Okay." She leans in and kisses my cheek. "Take the car. And bring me home a milkshake."

"Deal."

"And we need butter."

"Double deal." I grab her keys and head out the door.

Acknowledgments

As always, my gratitude goes out to the fabulous team at Orca for all their hard work on the covers and formatting, and a special thanks to Tanya Trafford for all of her efforts on Zack's story.

Natasha Deen is the author of several books for young people, including the Orca titles *Terminate* and *Across the Floor*. She lives in Edmonton, Alberta. For more information, visit natashadeen.com.

978-1-4598-1120-1 PB

Javvan can't get a job because of his
criminal record. When he finally does
find work, he somehow lands in more
trouble than before and is desperate to
find a way out.

Chapter One

I see my chances for a new life die in the eyes of the interviewer. It's always in their eyes. They go flat, lifeless. And it always happens toward the end of the interview. Doesn't matter that I have work experience or that I'm willing to do any job and put in long hours. Doesn't matter that I'm a good student and on the track team. They ask that fateful question, and I have to answer honestly.

That's when their eyes go dead. It's all, "Thank you, Mr. Malhotra. We'll call you."

They never do.

This interview's no different. Bike-courier job. After-school hours, weekend gigs. I could work around my mom's schedule, make sure there's always someone to take my little brother, Sammy, to his after-school stuff. I'd told all of this to the interviewer. She'd smiled, called me a good son.

Not always, but I don't tell her that.

Then she'd laughed, said the job was mine.

Just as I am breathing the tightness out of my chest, she says, "Oh, shoot. Last question." She rolls her eyes, as though it is an annoyance to have to ask me. "Have you ever been arrested for theft?"

"Yes."

The smile holds—she thinks I'm joking. When I don't say, "Gotcha," realization kicks in.

End of smiles. End of her thinking I'm a good son.

"What were you arrested for?"

"I stole a car."

"And you were convicted."

"Yes." I want to tell her more, but it's complicated to explain. Plus, it would make me look like I'm trying too hard to minimize what I've done.

She gives me a look like I just farted. "Thank you, Mr. Malhotra. We'll call you."

"No. Please. I made a mistake," I told her. "Got caught up with a dumb moment—" Stupid. Now I just look like I'm trivializing my choices. "It was a bad decision, and I regret it."

She's standing, ready to shove me out the door. Glancing around like my presence is dirtying her white furniture, white walls, white suit.

"Please. Mrs. O'Toole. Give me a chance." I stay seated, unwilling to budge. This is my twenty-second interview. My twenty-second rejection. If I could go back in time and *not* steal that stupid Lexus, I would. One idiot moment. One stupid choice, and my life's been screwed ever since.

Mrs. O'Toole sighs. Takes off her red glasses and rubs her eyes. "It's not me," she says. "It's our clients. There are sensitive documents that get shipped. We can't take the risk."

"But I didn't steal any files—it was a car—"

"Javvan."

I stop. Use of my first name means it's a for-sure no.

"I have a ton of kids who want this job." She gives me a pointed look. "A ton of kids who didn't steal and didn't get convicted."

Two more years, and my youth record gets wiped. It may as well be twenty years. This thing will never stop following me.

"I have another interview." Her expression is full of pity. "I'm sorry. Good luck—I'm sure someone else will hire you."

"Yeah," I mumble as I stand and head for the door. "That's what the last guy said."

orca soundings

For more information on all the books
in the Orca Soundings series, please visit
orcabook.com.